TEMPLE RUN

TAKE CONTROL OF THIS STORY
IF YOU DARE

™

GET READY TO
RUN FOR YOUR LIFE!

TEMPLE RUN

RUN FOR YOUR LIFE! ™

DOOM LAGOON

EGMONT
USA
New York

With special thanks to Myke Bartlett

EGMONT
We bring stories to life

First published in the United Kingdom by Egmont UK Limited, 2014
First published in the United States of America by Egmont USA, 2014
443 Park Avenue South, Suite 806
New York, NY 10016
Cover illustration by Jacopo Camagni
Interior illustrations by Artful Doodlers
Text & illustrations copyright © 2014 Imangi Studios, LLC
All Rights Reserved
1 3 5 7 9 8 6 4 2
www.ImangiStudios.com
www.egmontusa.com
ISBN 978-1-60684-572-1
eBook ISBN 978-1-60684-575-2

Stay safe online. Any website addresses listed in this book are correct at the
time of going to print. However, Egmont is not responsible for content
hosted by third parties. Please be aware that online content can be subject to
change and websites may contain content that is unsuitable for children. We
advise that all children be supervised when using the Internet.

As the engine roars, you cling tightly to the edge of your seat. The swamp buggy is bouncing wildly along muddy banks at the edge of a wide, flat lagoon. To make matters worse, Guy Dangerous is singing. You, he, and Scarlett Fox have been driving across the island for hours now, and the lagoon is getting more and more swampy.

It's an amazing place, beautiful and frightening at the same time. Trees hung with moss stretch their branches across your path. Alligators bask in the sun and slide into the water. Snakes glide past on mud banks and toads croak around murky pools. You wonder what it would be like to be stranded out here, miles from civilization.

Guy's voice isn't that bad, actually. He's singing some old song about sleepy lagoons and tropical moons. Scarlett, meanwhile, is listening to opera on her iPod and pretending she can't hear him.

"You're pretty quiet, kid!" Guy shouts at you.

2

"How are you feeling?"

"Excited!" you tell him.

"I bet you are! We'll make an ace treasure hunter of you yet."

As the buggy roars down the middle of a broad stretch of water, you see the shape of a boat in the far distance. You sit up. Is that the wreck you've come here to explore?

No—it's way too small, and it's floating upright on the water, instead of lying at an angle. This must be the houseboat where Scarlett's old friend Pedro Silva is putting you up for the night.

You close your eyes, remembering the crazy series of events that brought you here.

It all started with the legend of the wreck. Deep in the swamps, the stories say, lies the wreck of a riverboat, a vintage paddle steamer called the *Marie Laveau*. Long thought lost, it has now been located. You were amazed to discover that this long-lost vessel was actually your personal property!

You weren't entirely clear on how you came to

inherit this mysterious wreck, but it has something to do with an eccentric old great-aunt Beatrice, way back in the twisty branches of the family tree. She was the owner of the *Marie Laveau* and all its contents. Now the rights to the atmospheric old vessel have transferred to you.

Owning a wrecked steamboat didn't sound like much of a thrill on the face of it, but then you found a letter from Beatrice. The *Marie Laveau* had been carrying a very special cargo when it was wrecked, the letter claimed. On board was a priceless ceremonial mask.

4

"*I was the sole survivor of the* Marie Laveau," wrote Beatrice. "*I have never dared to retrieve the mask myself.*"

That mask, along with the rest of the wreck, now belongs to you. You've seen pictures of the mask, and while valuable, it sure is funny-looking. It's a strange monkey face, with empty eye sockets. Beatrice's letter insisted you entrust it to a museum— but you'll need to find it first! Besides, there was no telling what other treasures might be on board. You couldn't wait to get to that swamp and start exploring.

Of course, your parents wouldn't let you go. For some crazy reason, they thought it would be too dangerous. Talk about buzzkill!

That's when Guy Dangerous and Scarlett Fox stepped in. "We're research explorers," Scarlett told you, tucking a strand of red hair behind her ear. "My museum has been looking for the *Marie Laveau* for years. Let us accompany you and we'll keep you safe. Deal?"

Naturally, you said yes.

"It'll be educational and very perilous!" said Guy, grinning. Scarlett elbowed him in the ribs. "I mean, fun," he said, still grinning. "Extremely fun."

Now, as the buggy closes the distance to Pedro Silva's houseboat, your body hums with excitement. You're at the start of a great adventure.

"You do realize your old pal Silva's going to want to come along, too, right?" Guy yells.

Scarlett pops out one of her earbuds. "Don't be silly. He's retired."

"He says he's retired. I don't buy it. Nobody ever really gets out of the treasure-hunting game. Once it's in your blood . . ."

Scarlett laughs. "You're so suspicious! Relax, Guy. Pedro's a gentleman. Old-fashioned."

"Well, ain't that the truth," Guy mutters. "Old-fashioned. You said it."

You get your first glimpse of Pedro Silva when he comes out on deck and waves. He has dark hair streaked with gray and the most amazing beard you ever saw, long and pointy. His hat has a feather sticking out of it. Talk about dressing to impress.

"Scarlett!" Silva purrs. "So wonderful to see you again! And I see you brought your personal body-guard."

"Enjoying your retirement, Silva?" Guy growls. "Looks like you're getting a little tubby."

"And who is this?" Silva's gaze fixes on you. You feel those cold eyes sizing you up.

You introduce yourself. Silva gives a thoughtful nod. "Come aboard, *amigos*. Welcome."

Just as you're climbing onto the houseboat, the distant sound of a motor catches everyone's attention. Another swamp buggy is approaching.

Silva frowns. "I hope you have not invited more guests, Scarlett."

She shrugs. "Nothing to do with me!"

The other buggy pulls up. A well-muscled guy gets out and flashes a cop's badge.

"Officer Barry Bones," he says, looking at you. "You and me need to talk, bud."

"You and *me*?" you say, surprised.

"What's this about?" Guy demands, stepping in front of you protectively.

"None of your business," says Barry Bones. He turns to you again, keeping his voice down low. "We need to talk about the mask. I think you're in grave danger." You get the impression he's warning you not to trust the others. "Just know that I'm a friend, and that *I* want what *you* want—for the mask to end up in a museum. Not everyone does . . ."

Guy clenches his jaw . . . and his fist. "Sounds like you're accusing us of something, Officer."

The situation is getting tense.

To your relief, Silva steps in. "Why don't we all sit down to dinner? You, too, Officer Bones. It's all served, and it would be a shame to waste it."

Everyone, including Barry, grudgingly accepts.

Turn to page 8.

Although Silva is charming and welcomes everyone, you're convinced it's all a big act. He has mean-looking eyes, and there's something about him that makes you feel that he'd be more at home on the ocean waves, sailing some old-time pirate ship, than here in a houseboat on a swamp.

You shake the feeling off. You're probably just being silly. All this talk of treasure must be getting to you. Plus, Silva's a great cook. The fish he serves is done to perfection.

"So, now we are all friends, yes?" he says with a thin smile. "Let us talk about this wreck of yours. Surely you don't expect this mask still to be on board, after all these years? The wreck will have been picked clean by now."

You feel a thud of disappointment.

Barry Bones nods. "The mask's not there. But I know where it is."

"Sure you do," Guy snorts.

Silva pours you another glass of juice. "The mask is cursed, *amigo*. Did nobody tell you that?"

"No," you say. "But I'm not afraid of curses."

Silva laughs coldly. "I expect the crew of the *Marie Laveau* thought the same thing. At first. Did you ever hear the story of how the ship was lost?"

You know this story well. "There was a storm."

"That was the official story, yes." Silva taps his nose, which is pointy like his beard. "Nobody would have believed the truth."

"Which is?" says Barry.

"The *Marie Laveau* was set upon by demon monkeys. That is part of the curse of the mask."

Total silence. Scarlett clears her throat. Guy whistles. Barry looks awkward. Silva laughs as he clears the plates away. You have to wonder—did he really just say that? *Demon monkeys?* Are you stuck on a houseboat with a complete lunatic?

"So," Scarlett tells you across the table, "it's decision time. What's our next move?"

"We need to stick to our plan," Guy says. "Let's head out and explore the wreck as soon as we can. The

mask's in there. I can feel it in my, uh, bones." He gets up, adding that he's planning to camp on the banks of the swamp.

Barry Bones has other ideas. "You've got to trust me, buddy. I know that's a lot to ask. But stay here and you'll be in serious danger. I promise I'll explain more on the way." He nods at the others and leaves, gesturing for you to follow.

 Scarlett suppresses a yawn. "I suggest we enjoy Silva's hospitality for now, and make a decision in the morning," she says with a sleepy smile.

Silva nods. "Bad weather is on the way, and you do not want to be caught in a storm. Besides, the wreck has waited for you for many years, yes? It can wait a little longer."

To go with Guy's plan, turn to page 15.

If you trust Barry Bones, go to page 92.

To spend the night on the houseboat with Scarlett and Silva, head to page 17.

You're crawling through a tight and disgusting pipe. You stop suddenly as a web stretches across your face, and something large and leggy starts climbing up your face. It tiptoes down your neck and skitters along your spine. Then there's the smell. You're beginning to suspect this pipe is a sewer.

At what point did this seem like a good idea?

Still, at least you're going in the right direction. Ahead, you can see daylight. Unfortunately, you can also see a family of black rats. They're just hanging out, chatting among themselves. Until they see you, that is. One look in your direction and all six of them rush forward, nipping at your fingers with sharp yellow teeth. That's just unsanitary! You shriek and flap at the rats until, miraculously, you manage to scare them off.

Shuddering, you keep squeezing down the pipe until you come to a grille fitted into the roof. Using all your strength, you shove it free and heave yourself through the gap.

You stand up and discover that you're in the

heart of the temple, a broad chamber with a curved roof. A clear bolt of sunlight comes through a hole at its apex, spotlighting an altar in the center of the floor.

You've had some scares since you first started this crazy treasure hunt, but this is when your heart stops. There, resting on top of the stone altar, is the golden mask. You've found it!

Turn to page 101.

You dream of a demon monkey chasing you down a mountain. Its terrible screaming shakes the trees.

You wake up clutching at your sheets. It's a relief to see daylight in the portholes. All that talk about demon monkeys must have gotten to you. For a moment, you think you can still hear screaming.

Wait. You *can* still hear screaming. But this is a man, not a demon monkey. Maybe Guy's tent wasn't as gator-proof as he hoped!

You jump out of bed. The screaming is coming from upstairs. You recognize Silva's voice and wonder who he's shouting at.

As you get up on deck, you see Silva being bundled off the boat by a group of dark figures. For a second, you mistake the figures for demon monkeys, but the morning sun reveals that their strange, animal-like faces are just masks. No, not just masks—rough-and-ready copies of *the* mask, carved from old wood and embedded with gravel.

They have knives strapped to their bare legs and

crossbows belted across their backs. Silva is struggling against them, trying to avoid being dragged onto a waiting speedboat. He has his backpack, no doubt full of gems—*your* gems, from *your* wreck—slung over his shoulder.

There's no sign of Scarlett.

Do you rush to help Silva and rescue the treasure? Run to page 45.

Or do you stay where you are and hope the masked men won't notice you? Go to page 48.

Guy picks a spot on squishy ground, in the shadow of the wreck, and pitches his tent.

"Aren't you worried about gators?" you ask, glancing at the water's edge near the tent's screen door.

"I never worry about anything," Guy says. "Besides, this tent is gator-proof."

You raise an eyebrow at the flimsy canvas.

"Well, gator-resistant," Guy admits.

You wonder if it's too late to head back to the boat. But one look up at the wreck is enough to change your mind. It's almost ghostly, a relic of some bygone age of adventure and excitement. You can hear it creaking and trembling. If only it was morning already! You can't wait to start exploring.

You also can't wait to eat. Maybe you can get started on the cooking while Guy wrestles with the tent. "Is the food in your backpack?" you ask.

"What food? Explorers don't *carry* food. If you get stuck in quicksand, the last thing you want is a can of Spam dragging you down."

"Then what are we going to eat?"

Guy puts a heavy hand on your shoulder and grins. "The question is, what *aren't* we going to eat? But food isn't important right now."

Your stomach rumbles loudly in disagreement.

"Think," he says. "What's most important to an explorer?"

You sigh. "Um. Water?" you suggest.

"Smart. Now, we've got two options. We can head farther into the swamp and see what turns up. Or you can fill up the collapsible bucket here."

The murky water is sucking at your feet. "Where's the bucket?" you ask.

"Here," he says, passing it to you. "But watch out, that's a muddy shore you're standing on. You'll need to wade out pretty deep, otherwise you'll be bringing back a bucket of dirt."

To wade in with the bucket, turn to page 23.

To search for water, go to page 37.

The houseboat is great! The food is good, the cabin is warm, and Silva tells a few more weird stories about shipwrecked ghosts and demon monkeys.

You want to stay up late, but you're exhausted. It's been a long journey getting this far, and tomorrow will be a big day. You head to bed, dreaming of treasure.

Walking down to your bunk, you pass Silva's room. His door has been left ajar.

You know it's wrong to poke around in someone else's stuff, but something doesn't sit right about Silva. What's he doing here in the swamp, so close to the wreck, if he really isn't interested in the *Marie Laveau*?

You creep into his cabin. There is a small bed with a lush red velvet bedspread, a narrow wooden wardrobe, and a solid oak writing desk. The top of the desk is plastered with an ancient map of the world and an old two-way radio on top. There's nothing in the wardrobe but some puffy shirts.

Ah well. You're about to give up when you spot a dusty old chest under the desk, shoved against the cabin wall. You pull it out, wiping away some of the dirt on the lid. There's a faded label, and it reads: *Marie Laveau*.

Opening the box, you find that it's full of precious gems. Silva has been on board your wreck! No wonder he told you it was picked clean.

You hear footsteps. Someone is coming down the stairs. You're holding gems in your hands. This could be awkward to explain.

If you choose to hide, turn to page 21.

If you take a deep breath and face whoever it is, head to page 26.

The air inside the mine is cold and tastes like old smoke. Didn't miners once keep canaries to let them know if their mine had a gas leak? That's one thing you didn't think to pack!

"Check that out," Barry says, shining his flashlight at some marks in the dust by your boots. "Somebody else has been here recently, maybe in the last day or two."

You're about to ask who, when a hurled dagger whizzes past you. It sparks against the jagged rocks of the mine wall. You drop into a crouch and peer out around the side of the entrance. Then you wish you hadn't. A dozen figures with hunched shoulders and evil-looking skull faces are scrambling out of the bushes.

"Demon monkeys!" you gasp.

Pedro Silva was right!

A second later you realize their skull faces are masks, carved from wood. They're just men after all. Sadly, the long knives in their hands are all too real.

Barry tenses beside you. "They *really* don't want us getting that mask," he mutters. "Let's move!"

Barry's ready to run deeper into the mine, but you remember the pulley system you saw outside. You could ride that down the hill to safety.

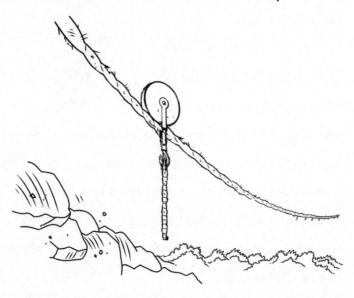

To shelter in the mine, turn to page 46.

To fly down the hill with the pulley system, turn to page 57.

You consider ducking under the desk. Wait. If Silva decides to sit down, he'll have to rest his boots on your head . . . and there's no room under the bed . . . So it'll have to be the wardrobe.

The door clicks shut behind you. You swear you can hear your heart beating. You wouldn't be surprised if Silva could, too.

The footsteps enter the room, pause, and then fade away. *Phew!*

You wait a minute and then give the wardrobe door a shove.

It doesn't budge.

You shove harder.

It still doesn't move, but the floor does.

You've triggered some sort of trapdoor, which sends you plummeting into the dark water below the boat. The water is warm, but it's too murky to see anything. You try to feel your way to port side or starboard, but you can't tell which way you're going. Something brushes your leg. Something that feels a *lot* like an alligator.

There's probably a lesson here about snooping around in someone else's things. Bad news is, you won't have time to learn it. *Chomp!*

RUN AGAIN? TURN TO PAGE **8**

You wade into the swampy water with Guy's bucket. Why is he carrying a collapsible bucket around with him, anyway? What's wrong with a water bottle?

You haven't made it far when the ground turns to mush beneath your boots. Slime squeezes in around your heels and soaks your socks. It feels disgusting, and the water gets deep quickly.

Something moves in the swamp ahead of you. In the moonlight, you glimpse an eye glaring at you. To your left, something long and bumpy slides beneath the water. Best not to hang around.

The water looks clear enough here. You fill the bucket to the brim and start heading back to

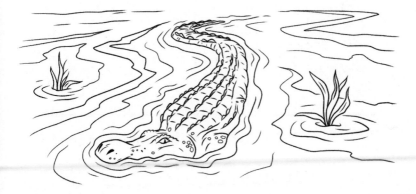

24

shore. It's heavier than you thought it would be.

Behind you, you hear the alligators swishing around. You get the feeling they're following you.

You try to run, but the mud pulls at your legs. The faster you try to move, the deeper you sink. The water ripples around you. The gators are closing in.

You realize you could probably run faster if you ditched the bucket. On the other hand, you've carried it this far—what's a little farther?

To keep the bucket, turn to page 65.

To ditch the bucket, turn to page 75.

You slide on after Guy. Soon you're moving too quickly to grab hold of anything. The rush of water becomes even more furious. You crash through doors and bounce down open chutes. Finally, the floor gives way and you tumble into wet darkness.

"Guess we hit bottom," Guy says, spitting water.

You take his word for it. There's nothing to see. You're paddling furiously to keep afloat. Overhead, more swamp water pours in through the hole you just fell through. This doesn't look good.

"Don't panic," says Guy. "This kind of thing happens all the time."

"Seriously?"

"Sure. We just need to do exactly what I did back in Kathmandu and—" Guy's about to tell you exactly what he did back in Kathmandu when the whole ship collapses on top of you. Now you'll never know. As if dying wasn't bad enough!

RUN AGAIN? TURN TO PAGE **8**

26

The cabin door swings open, but it isn't Silva.

"What on earth are you doing?" Scarlett whispers, looking back toward the stairs.

You want to ask her the same thing. "I got lost."

Scarlett arches an eyebrow. "Is that right?"

"OK, I was having a quick look around," you admit. "And it's good I did! He's got a trunk of treasure from the *Marie Laveau*!"

You swear Scarlett looks hungry. "Treasure? What treasure?"

You tell her about the gems and she seems mildly disappointed. "You're sure the mask wasn't in there?"

"I'm sure. Do you think this means there's more treasure left on board?"

Scarlett nods. "Old Pedro wouldn't still be weighing anchor here if he thought he'd found all of it." She pats your shoulder. "Well done."

"I thought you'd be mad I was snooping."

Scarlett purses her lips. You get the feeling she's sizing you up. "In my experience, being a treasure hunter sometimes requires a bit of sneakiness."

In *her* experience? Sounds like there is definitely more to Scarlett than meets the eye.

"Maybe we should call Barry Bones," you suggest. "Those gems are mine, after all. He stole them from my wreck!"

"Don't be ridiculous," Scarlett snaps, then composes herself. "I mean, it's the middle of the night. If we confront Pedro about this now, he'll be furious. I don't want to spend the night camped in a gator-resistant tent with Guy. Let's sleep on it and talk again in the morning."

"But—"

"Shh!" Scarlett puts a finger to her lips and nods toward the stairs. You can hear the floorboards creaking above you. Is Pedro listening? "In the morning," Scarlett whispers.

You go to bed grumpy. Even the soft cotton sheets can't cheer you up. Maybe Scarlett isn't so great after all. There's something not quite right about her.

You wake up before you even realize you've

fallen asleep. Someone is moving around in the darkness. "Scarlett?" you whisper. "Is that you?"

There's no reply. Whoever is moving stops, just for a second. Then you feel the boat rock gently again in time with their movements.

Maybe it's Silva. Do you want to confront him now about stealing your treasure? Or should you stay in bed, like Scarlett suggested?

To go see if it's Silva, turn to page 40.

To stay in bed, go to page 13.

The path zigzags up the mountain. In places, the undergrowth spills over in piles of knotted green. Trees have fallen and been left to rot. It doesn't look like anybody has been here in years.

You're just setting off up the slope when a piercing scream sounds from the top of the mountain. The sun is hot on the back of your neck, yet you still shiver.

But nothing's going to stop you from getting your hands on that mask. Not now. You feel it drawing you up the path, like it has a rope tied around your waist.

The hike is long and difficult. The farther you make it, the worse the path gets. Stones come loose beneath your feet, sending you tumbling backward. You have to pull apart prickly bushes and clamber over ant-infested logs. At one point, you jump clear of a bright yellow snake that drops down from an overhanging branch.

Looking to your left, you can hear the rumble of a waterfall. Hoping for some fresh water, you leave the path and push through a thicket of trees.

You find yourself at the bottom of a steep rock face with a waterfall gushing down it. At the top of the mountain is the temple!

The rock face is ragged. It might be easier to climb here than continuing to tear through the overgrown path.

On the other hand, that's hundreds of feet of rock you'll be scaling, without any equipment.

To climb the rock face, go to page 98.

To return to the path, go to page 107.

"Here, I'll give you a leg up!" Guy drops the trunk, gets on one knee, and makes a sling with his hands. Taking a deep breath, you run toward him and plant your right foot in his palm-sling. He flings you up into the air. You manage to grab hold of the edge of the lifeboat and pull yourself into it.

"Don't forget this!"

You peer down just in time to see Guy throw the treasure chest at you. It crashes beside you, causing the boat to swing wildly in its moorings. Doubloons spill and rattle around the wooden deck.

Guy leaps at the boat and hauls himself up. "Here!" he says, thrusting his knife at you. "You'll have to cut the ropes. And quick!"

You grab the knife and look up. The lifeboat is fastened to the overhead girder by a strong-looking rope.

Guy has dragged himself into the boat. "Hurry up. And don't forget to hold on tight."

Below, you can see the ship's deck collapsing

under the weight of the rain. Any second now, the *Marie Laveau* will fold in on itself. You hack at the rope with the knife—

The lifeboat tears free. You throw yourself forward, next to Guy. Too late, you realize the boat isn't going to drop into the water. Instead, the lifeboat hits the deck with a massive *thwack!* It careens across what's left of the boards, bounces off the chimney stack, and then crashes through the rail to shoot out over the swamp.

For a moment, silence. Then you hit the water with such force it knocks you unconscious.

★

You wake up the next morning, lying on a muddy riverbank. The sun is glaring from a clear blue sky. That's the first thing you notice. The second thing is that you're surrounded by gators.

"Haiiiiii!"

Guy rushes into the water, waving his arms around and shouting. It freaks out the gators about as much as it does you. While he's doing that, you scurry up the bank and clamber up the first tree you find.

Ten seconds later, Guy joins you. "Well," he says. "We're alive, which is good news."

Farther down the bank, you can see what's left of the *Marie Laveau*—little more than a pile of rusted iron, submerged at the muddy edge of a swamp. You feel a little sad about this, and try not think about what treasures have been lost to a muddy grave. Wait a minute—treasure!

You look down at the lifeboat, resting on its side at the water's edge.

"Where's all the gold?" you ask.

Guy looks sheepish. "Sorry, that's the bad news. It all went overboard when we hit the water."

"All of it?"

"Well, not quite." He pulls something from his pocket and throws it at you. Opening your hand, you find a single gold doubloon.

"Call it a souvenir," Guy says.

So much for being rich. But at least you'll have something to show the kids at school. Not that you expect anyone to believe your story.

Still, as Guy starts charting a course back to civilization, you wonder whether the mask really did sink to the bottom of the swamp. Maybe Barry Bones was right instead. Maybe it's hidden somewhere else.

But you guess you'll never know . . .

RUN AGAIN? TURN TO PAGE **8**

Barry helps you into one of the carts, releases the brake, and you start rolling. You quickly pick up speed, but the tunnel is way too dark to see any distance ahead of you. Standing up to peer over Barry's shoulder, you just manage to duck a low wooden beam.

"Follow my lead," Barry says, leaning to the left.

You wonder what he's doing, and then you see the switch in the tracks. The shaft again forks in two, but the right shaft is blocked by a rock fall. You lean hard left, just in time. The cart swings around the corner. That was way too close!

"Lean right, lean right!" Barry shouts.

This time you don't even look. It's only as you whizz safely into another shaft that you see the boards hammered across the tracks turning left.

Still, this is one heck of a roller coaster. When you get to the bottom, you might go back to the top. If you get to the bottom alive, that is.

"OK, buddy. Time to grab hold of that brake."

As you move to take hold of the lever at the

back of the cart, a crossbow bolt grazes the back of your hand. The demon monkey men are behind you, riding in another cart! You can just make out one of them reloading his crossbow.

"Hey! Are you listening back there? We need to slow down, pronto! There's a steep bend ahead and I don't want us coming off the rails."

Another bolt whizzes past, zinging off the walls. You don't want to give that sniper a better shot.

**To brake and try to stay on the tracks,
go to page 96.**

To try to outrun the thieves, go to page 42.

Y ou and Guy press into the swamp. The undergrowth is thick, with sharp branches and prickly leaves. Huge vines drape from the swollen branches of the mangroves. While you're busy watching your feet, one of the vines—actually, a snake!—wraps itself under your chin like a noose and lifts you off the ground. Guy snatches the knife he keeps strapped to his leg and slashes you free.

"Eyes and ears. Danger is everywhere." He looks way too happy about that.

"I guess that's why Scarlett prefers the houseboat lifestyle," you say, thinking of her, most likely smug and indoors.

"Don't you worry about Scarlett," Guy

says, and you think he looks a little angry. "She's *very* good at looking after number one."

You wonder what this means. Should you be wary of Scarlett? Is she here to help herself, and not you after all?

After a while, Guy perks up again. As you walk, he points out a long list of hazards. Snakes, gator holes, spider nests, quicksand, swamp gas, ant mounds, poisonous berries, bloodsucking bats. By the time he's finished, you're expecting to die at any moment.

You come to a clearing. Guy stops. "Let's use that brain of yours. We're lost deep in the swamp—"

Your eyes widen. "We're *lost?*"

"This is an exercise, kid. I'm going to teach you to survive out here. So how do we go about finding fresh water?"

You think quickly. You're in the wilderness, surrounded by deadly creatures. But even they need to drink, right? "We follow an animal," you say.

Guy's face lights up and he slaps you on the back.

Then he helps you up from the bush you've fallen into. "A plus. So let's find a thirsty beast."

You and Guy look around for animals to follow. Something rustles in a nearby tree. In the moonlight, you catch sight of a pale, cheeky face peering down at you.

"A monkey!" you say. "We can follow a monkey."

Guy doesn't look convinced. "Any amateur can follow a monkey," he says. "This is way more exciting!" He's pointing at a fat, dark-furred bee that is buzzing in circles around his head.

To insist on chasing the monkey, run to page 73.

To buzz after the bee, go to page 114.

The noise is coming from Silva's cabin. You peer through the crack in his door and see him inside, crouching on the floor. He's stuffing an old-style backpack with the treasure from the box. The treasure your great-aunt wanted *you* to find.

"That's *mine!*" you blurt out, swinging open the door.

Silva stands up in shock. You worry he's going to pull his sword from his scabbard and run you through with it. You'll probably die of some weird, old-fashioned disease. Or maybe just from a sword wound in the gizzard.

Thankfully, his sword stays where it is. So does your gizzard.

Silva holds up both of his hands. "This isn't what it looks like, my young friend. Go back to bed. I will explain everything when you wake."

"So you're not running off with all the gems in the middle of the night? Because that's what it looks like."

"No, no. Why would I abandon such a fine vessel as this?" He shakes his head vigorously. "There are thieves about, *amigo*. I am merely taking precautions. Go back to bed, for your own good."

Maybe it's just his tone, but that sounds a lot like a threat.

You're not sure you're convinced, but maybe you should listen to a man with a sword. Turn to page 13.

On the other hand, Scarlett might know what to do. To shout and wake her, go to page 62.

Y ou don't touch the brake. With you and Barry leaning right out of the cart, you just manage to cling to the rails.

Sparks fly as you careen around the curve and plunge into another tunnel. You're picking up even more speed. The cart is rattling and the wind is whipping at your hair.

"I think we lost them!" you shout, looking behind you and seeing nothing.

"Good work!" Barry shouts back.

The track rises up and your stomach lurches. Then, at the top of the slope, the track disappears! A section has fallen into an open chasm.

The cart shoots into the air, then crashes down on the far side of the gap. You spill out, scraped and grazed from the tunnel floor.

When you sit up, you're astonished to find the only thing you've broken is your flashlight.

Barry isn't so lucky. "Think my ankle's busted," he says, wincing. "I'm not going anywhere."

A thundering rattle clatters down the tunnel behind you. Those demon monkey men are still in pursuit! Luckily, they've been more cautious. Their cart isn't moving anywhere near as quickly as yours was. It rattles off the end of the rails and plummets down into the chasm. You hear their screams and then a crash. Then, silence.

"That won't be the last of them," Barry says.

"There'll be more coming for us. We're sitting ducks."

You look down the tunnel. You can see a faint green glow. You remember what Barry said about the mask having special properties. Maybe the mask really is here.

Barry pulls a shortwave radio from his pocket. His hands are shaking too much to operate it. The radio drops to the ground and you pick it up.

"Someone out there's got to hear us," Barry says.

Do you stay with Barry to help him radio for backup? Or should you press on down the tunnel, in the hope of finding that mask?

To stay with Barry, turn to page 63.

To go on alone, turn to page 104.

You charge at the attackers. The man closest to you spins around in a panic and falls overboard. That's a pretty good start!

You're just about to congratulate yourself when another man swipes you with the back of his hand, knocking you along the deck.

You crash into the wood paneling. If this were a cartoon, there would be birds twittering all around your head.

"Leave the kid!" one of the attackers shouts. "It's the woman we want. She too has evil plans!"

Evil plans? you think. *Scarlett?*

One of the men snatches his crossbow from his back and hurries downstairs, below deck. Should you go and warn Scarlett, or stay here and fight?

To try to warn Scarlett, turn to page 51.

To stay and fight, turn to page 56.

You and Barry sprint off along the tight shaft, deeper into the mine. You can hear the masked men following you, their threatening voices echoing along the dark walls.

"Stay with me!" Barry shouts back at you. "We can lose these suckers."

You're not so sure. It's too dark to see where you're going. Any second now, you'll trip and splatter yourself on the tracks.

Suddenly, Barry grinds to a halt and you slam into his back.

You've reached a fork in the road. Two shafts lead away into darkness. For all you know, one shaft could lead to a dead end. You'd be trapped.

"What are they going to do . . . if they catch us?" you whisper, glancing between the two shafts.

"Well," Barry says, "they're not going to take us home to meet their mama. Hey, would you look at that?"

Shining his flashlight down the left shaft reveals a pair of coal carts, sitting on shaky-looking rails.

Barry grins. "Welcome to the Bones Express!"

"This way might be safer," you say, peering down the other shaft. You'd have to go on foot, and it looks narrower, *and* the roof is sagging, but maybe that's still better than a wild cart-ride through pitch-darkness?

To ride the Bones Express, hop to page 35.

To squeeze down the other shaft,
go to page 151.

The thieves' boat vanishes into the distance, taking Silva with it. His shouts echo through the mangrove trees, startling some brightly colored birds.

Scarlett isn't anywhere on the houseboat. When did she leave? Maybe she's gone off to explore the wreck on her own. So much for working together!

You head back to Silva's quarters, hoping to use the two-way radio, but you can't get it working. Looking closely, you see that the map of the world is attached to the desk only by Scotch tape. It's covering something up! One edge of the map is dog-eared, as if it has been lifted up quite recently.

Beneath the map, the desktop is plain wood, but something has been carved into it. You recognize the outline of the island and, yes, there is the swamp and a drawing of the *Marie Laveau*. Silva must have dragged this whole desk off your wreck. A rough line leads from the ship toward what looks like a temple, deep in the swamp. Maybe Scarlett saw this and went looking.

You're about to make a copy of the map when Barry Bones pulls up in his buggy.

"I decided to try again," he says. "I really want you to come with me."

You tell him Silva has been kidnapped by masked thieves. Barry doesn't look surprised.

"And Scarlett's gone," you say. "I think she's looking for the mask in a temple in the mountains."

"The mask isn't in any temple," Barry says. "But I know where it *is* hiding. And I could do with a partner on this case. You up to it?"

If you're ready to go with Barry, turn to page 92.

If you'd rather copy that map and go find the temple, turn to page 29.

You take a deep breath and sprint toward the jets of fire. Just when you can feel the flame singe your eyebrows, you drop onto your back and slide. The fire roars overhead. You've made it!

Unfortunately, that gas seam ran deep. Three more spurts of fire spit from the tunnel floor ahead of you. These jets are too high to jump, but every now and then they splutter. Maybe you can leap through the fire, if you get your timing right. That would be a cool story to tell.

To brave the flames, run to page 141.

To retreat and try the other tunnel, head to page 111.

You charge down the stairs after the thief, but you're in such a rush, you forget to duck.

Thunk!

★

When you wake up, you're in a hospital on the other side of the island. A TV is flickering at the foot of the bed, playing an episode of Guy Dangerous's adventure series, *Whatever It Takes*. There's Guy, about to wrestle a bear, when he turns to the camera and says something—in Spanish!

You hear a sigh from beside the bed.

"They never get the voice right when they dub these things. I sound way more heroic in real life."

Guy is sitting in a chair beside you, frowning at the screen. Seeing that you're awake, he gives you a broad smile.

"You gave me a scare, kid. Lucky I came back to check on you."

You try to sit up. The mask is still out there. So is Scarlett. And your treasure.

Guy leans over, holding you back. "No more

adventures for you. Doctor's orders. You're on the first flight home. Better leave the exploring to the professionals, eh?"

You try to argue, but you've got the world's biggest headache. This really wasn't the ending you had in mind.

RUN AGAIN? TURN TO PAGE 8

Your arm nearly comes loose from your shoulder, but you manage to cling to an open doorway.

As he rockets away, Guy yells at you to keep going. "Don't worry about me. Meet you at the—"

But the rush of rainwater drowns him out. *The tent? Pedro's houseboat? The shore?!*

As Guy slides out of sight, you pull yourself up into a cabin and hurry across to its porthole. The glass is already broken, so you jump through and drop down to the muddy bank.

There's a horrible groan of metal behind you, and you run as fast as you can into the undergrowth as the wreck finally collapses in on itself. Debris smacks into the shore, crushing the tent and the rest of your supplies. You hope Guy made it out safely. Surely, if anyone could, he could. Maybe he'll even save that treasure of yours!

Thunk!

You've run headfirst into a mangrove tree. Lucky you have a hard head!

54

Suddenly everything is looking a bit woozy . . .

Hours pass in a hot, dizzy haze. You keep stumbling along, but your brain is so fuzzy you have trouble remembering why you're in this wet, sticky swamp to begin with. Eventually, it comes to you that you were here with some people—a guy named Guy, and a woman named Scarlett. But you can't be sure. And anyway, where are they now?

Finally, you collapse, exhausted. You're expecting to be met by soft, swampy earth, but instead your face smacks against cold stone. That's enough of a jolt to wake you up.

Somehow, you've arrived at the foot of a mountain. From here, a stone path leads up through the undergrowth toward a strange, ancient-looking structure. Wreathed in vines, it looks like some kind of temple.

You're not sure you're ready for a steep climb. Not when your brain feels like a marshmallow. But then you notice a circular pattern set into the stone wall of the path.

It looks so familiar, and suddenly everything comes back to you. You're supposed to be finding a *mask*. Could it be hidden here?

Turn to page 29.

You headbutt one attacker, knocking him overboard, and manage to trip another, sending him crashing into Silva's dinghy.

But in the end you're outnumbered. You're sent sprawling across the deck as they drag Silva aboard their boat and set off across the swamp.

"Wimps!" you shout after them.

That's your treasure they're making off with! You jump down onto Guy's buggy, which he left behind. The controls look simple. Squinting into the sun reflecting on the swamp, you spot the thieves' boat and press down hard on the accelerator.

Unfortunately, the buggy is still tied to Silva's boat. As you rev the engine, it swings around into the hull with a massive crash, busting the buggy's front tire.

Turn to page 48.

You dart back outside, straight at your attackers.

"Are you crazy?" Barry shouts, chasing after you.

A knife flies past your head and nicks your left ear. Ouch. You jump into the empty coal cart at the top of the conveyor. Your weight kick-starts the mechanism and soon you're zooming off down the side of the hill. *"Woo-hooooo!"*

Something thuds into the bottom of your cart. A crossbow bolt. The attackers aren't letting you get away that easily. Barry is in the cart behind you. He ducks as another bolt streaks through the air. This time, it falls short.

You've made a clean getaway. *Almost.* All fast rides have to end some time. And this ride ends in a spinning metal wheel at the bottom of the hill. You guess it was designed to knock the coal from its cart. Best not to guess what it might do to you.

To jump out of the cart, turn to page 90.

Or hey, let's be optimistic! Maybe you'll pass safely through. To stay in, skip to page 85.

A s dawn breaks over the swamp, you get your first good look at the wreck. The hull is rusted and worn through in several large patches, but it's still a thing of beauty. "Maybe we could climb in through one of the holes?" you suggest.

"Good thinking."

Guy jogs down the bank until he finds a rusted gash large enough for the two of you to squeeze into. You're about to climb in when Guy grabs your shoulder and holds you back.

"Just remember. Between rust, metal fatigue, and who-knows-what living on board, this ship is a deathtrap. The whole thing could collapse any minute." He grins. "Remembering that should make the whole thing way more exciting!"

Guy dives headfirst through the hole in the hull. From inside, you hear a faint whoop and a splash. You climb through with more care, trying not to cut yourself on the sharp metal. As you drop down into waist-deep water, you reach for your pocket flashlight. You seem to be in the engine room. To your left, vast turbines and pistons appear in the light, like the bones of some prehistoric creature.

Guy whistles at the engine, impressed, but is soon looking at his boots. "The rain's getting heavy," he says. "The water's rising. We can't hang around."

You trudge after him through the dark water, hoping nothing nasty is living in it. Because the ship is tilted toward shore, the floor is on an angle. You're climbing uphill, but at least the water is getting shallower.

Reaching the engine room door, Guy puts his hand on the knob and then stands back with a grin. "It's your wreck. After you!"

You push past him eagerly. This is it. Treasure awaits. You yank the door open. It seems you were *too* eager, because the whole ship starts to shudder! The floor gives way beneath you.

"Run!" Guy shouts.

You sprint up the sloping corridor. Behind you, a section of roof collapses with a loud crash, blocking your exit.

"Faster, kid, faster!"

Looking ahead, you see rotten panels are dropping away from the corridor floor. You speed up and throw yourself across the gap. It's close, and you've only just found your feet when you need to jump again.

A steel girder comes loose from a wall, falling across your path. You drop onto your back and slide beneath it, ducking your head. Lucky you're running so fast!

Ahead, the corridor comes to a sharp turn and continues off to your left. There's also a ladder on the wall right ahead of you, leading to the level above. Maybe the floor will be sturdier there?

To climb the ladder, turn to page 82.

To take the corridor, turn to page 119.

"Scarlett, wake up!" you yell.

There's no response. As you turn around to call out again, Silva rushes past, shoving you hard against the door frame, and disappears up the stairs.

You hurry to Scarlett's cabin, but it's empty. The bed doesn't look slept in. Maybe she crept off during the night to find the mask on her own. Maybe that's Silva's plan, too!

Running up to the deck, you're just in time to see Silva leap onto the swamp buggy. Moments later, he's burning away across the swamp.

You remember the small dinghy attached to the houseboat. The problem is, it's no longer attached to the houseboat. Silva has cut the rope and the dinghy's drifting away. If you jump now, you might just make it. But maybe chasing after Silva is a bad idea. It's still dark, and this is a job for a policeman. You remember seeing the radio on Silva's desk.

Do you use the radio to call Barry Bones for help? Turn to page 66.

Or chase Silva yourself? Go to page 142.

You try radioing for help, but all you hear is static. You try your phone, but there's no signal. That figures. There's who-knows-how-many feet of solid rock between you and open air. You might as well whistle.

"Stay there," you tell Barry.

He doesn't find this funny.

You run back to the chasm and crawl to its edge. You can't see the bottom, but the cut runs wide, slicing through the tunnel walls on either side. Maybe it runs all the way to the outside.

"Help!" you shout into the chasm. "*HELP!*"

You listen. The echo of your voice shouts back at you.

When you look up, there are six masked men staring down at you from the other side of the chasm. Knives and crossbows are pointing in your direction. While you're getting to your feet, one of the men takes a running leap, vaults the chasm, and drops down beside you.

OK. You're probably wondering what these

men want. And what's with those demon monkey masks, anyway?

We might as well tell you, since you won't be sticking around. Basically, you're about to be sacrificed to their demon monkey god. This isn't going to be pleasant, so let's look away now . . .

RUN AGAIN? TURN TO PAGE 8

Soon you're up to your waist in mud. "Help!" Guy hears your cries and quickly throws you a rope. "Grab hold!" he shouts. "Pull yourself free!"

Holding the bucket with one hand, you grasp the rope with the other—but it slips through your fingers. Clenching your teeth, you do your best to yank yourself free from the mud.

"Hold on tight," Guy says. "I'll get you out!"

He gives the rope a sharp tug, but again it flies right through your hand.

Let's face it, you're stuck. The only thing strong enough to pull you free is the gator behind you. That's good news for the gator. Not such good news for you.

Crunch!

RUN AGAIN? TURN TO PAGE **8**

In Silva's cabin, you find the radio smashed. There's no way of getting in touch with Barry now. Thinking you might be able to sail the houseboat to safety, you run up to the stern—but the engine won't start. You discover the motor has been trashed. An ax lies beside the wreckage.

Looks like Silva has no plans on returning. You have the feeling Scarlett won't be back, either.

You, on the other hand, are going nowhere. The dinghy is long gone and you don't fancy swimming to shore through gator-infested waters.

Guess you could be waiting here a while to be rescued. Still, at least you'll have plenty of time to wonder what you could have done differently.

RUN AGAIN? TURN TO PAGE **8**

You fly through the air and grab the edge of the buggy, just managing to pull yourself up.

"That's far enough, Silva," you say. "That's stolen property you're carrying!"

Silva spins around. Keeping one hand on the wheel, he uses the other to smooth his impressive beard. "You are very brave, *amigo*. But Pedro Silva is a champion swordsman!"

His hand goes to his belt, but his sword is gone! In the hustle and bustle of the chase, he's dropped it on the buggy floor. You snatch up his fallen sword and jab it toward him.

Silva raises his hands in surrender. "You have bested me, *amigo*."

You're just about to demand Silva hand over the gems when he leaps down into the dinghy, taking your treasure with him. Laughing, he restarts the motor and tears away across the swamp.

You drop down into the buggy's driving seat, put the pedal to the metal, and chase after him. But the buggy is too slow to keep up.

Silva pulls out a fistful of gems and holds it aloft, gloating. "You think you are a match for the great Pedro Silva?"

Gah. His habit of referring to himself in the third person is *really* irritating.

"He once bested the great Cortés himself! He outsmarted the Viceroy of Cuba! Pedro Silva is a living legend who—"

You never find out the rest of that sentence. Silva is so busy showing off that he isn't looking where he's going. The prow of the dinghy slams into a large submerged log, flinging Silva through the air. You watch as he crashes down into a nest of gators, taking the gems with him. The last you hear from him, he is challenging the largest alligator to a duel.

★

Shortly afterward, Barry Bones arrives in his swamp buggy. Guy is sitting beside him. "Had a feeling you might be in trouble," Barry says.

Guy shakes his head. "This isn't trouble, this is adventure!"

"Listen, buddy, I know you wanted to explore the wreck," Barry says to you. "But the mask's not there, anyway. Come with me and we'll find it together."

"That wreck still has its secrets," Guy insists. "If that mask is anywhere, it'll be on board. Besides, it'll be far more *fun* to explore than some lousy old mineshaft." He grins and eagerly rubs his hands together.

If you decide to go to the wreck with Guy, turn to page 58.

If you'd rather go with Barry, turn to page 92.

"You're a hero!" Barry Bones slaps you on the back. Somehow you manage to keep hold of the mask. In the hotel lobby, you tell him all about how Scarlett behaved at the temple.

Barry just nods, like you're confirming his suspicions. "She's really slippery, that Scarlett," he says. "Now, what about you?"

You look at the mask in your hands. It feels like it's staring back at you. Judging you.

"This deserves to be in a museum," you say reluctantly, handing Barry the mask. "That's the safest place."

Barry grins. "Like I said, bud. You're a hero."

You call your parents to tell them the good news. You'll fly home tomorrow. Retelling your adventures, you get the feeling they don't quite believe you. You can't blame them. It's been an incredible couple of days.

★

Months later, you take some friends to see the mask in the museum. It looks stunning in its new glass case. There's a little plaque with your name on it, explaining

that you donated it. You tell your friends all about the wild expedition when you rescued the mask from an ancient temple. None of them believes you.

Ah well. Even if nobody else believes you, you know what you've done. But then you start thinking. What didn't you do? What other adventures might have been waiting for you if you'd made a few different choices?

RUN AGAIN? TURN TO PAGE 8

Seeing you beside him, Silva speeds up. The spray from his tires stings your eyes and you cough up dirty water. That's *it*. You're not letting him get away from you now.

You rev the dinghy's engine as hard as you can. It starts spluttering thick black smoke. Silva swerves toward another islet, but you manage to keep on his tail. Faster. Faster.

Too fast! The engine overheats and bursts into flames. You jump back, startled, and lose control of the dinghy.

The vessel swerves out of control and crashes into a tree.

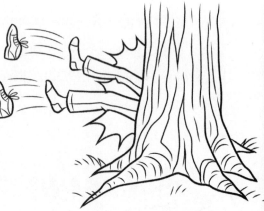

Oops! Who left that there?

RUN AGAIN? TURN TO PAGE 8

You and Guy follow the monkey farther inland. It swings nimbly from treetop to treetop, but always stays in view. When you fall into a gator hole and Guy spends a minute explaining its features before pulling you free, the monkey waits in the nearest tree for you to catch up.

"Maybe it's a friendly monkey," you suggest. "Aren't there stories of dolphins helping castaways back safely to land?"

"You can't trust a dolphin," Guy says. "I'd rather swim with sharks any day. Hey, did you watch that episode of *Whatever It Takes* where I punched a tiger shark?"

You follow the monkey into a thick clump of mangroves. Pushing quickly between the scaly trunks, you stumble into another clearing. The ground here is trodden and hard. A grove of trees encircles you like a high, curving wall. Eyes stare out from every tree. You can hear the chattering of high-pitched monkey voices.

Guy looks around at them with interest. "This is

unusual behavior for monkeys," he says. "It's almost like they've got us surrounded."

You have to agree. "This place looks like an *arena*," you whisper.

That's the last clever thought you have. The monkeys swoop down from overhead, knocking you and Guy to the ground.

You've been so busy wondering what monkeys drink, you haven't given any thought to what they eat. Here's a clue: they eat anything careless enough to follow them home. Is that a bit hard to swallow? Let's hope you make a leathery meal!

RUN AGAIN? TURN TO PAGE **8**

You drop the bucket and right away you can feel yourself lift in the mud. Soon your feet are coming away easily from the soggy bottom of the swamp. You splash through the water and make it back to shore with all your limbs intact. The gator lurking behind you seems to lose interest. Maybe it sees Guy standing above you, clapping his hands together, ready for a wrestle. Even a gator knows not to mess with Guy Dangerous.

"So much for the easy option," Guy says, helping you up onto your feet. "Let's get hiking. I've got a killer thirst coming on."

Head to page 37.

Using rocks from the water's edge, you help to smash open the log, exposing the waxy combs of the hive within. Bees swarm all around you. You wince, waiting for the first sting.

"Wake up," Guy says. "We're still alive and kicking. Mason bees only sting if you squash them."

He tears big chunks of honeycomb from the hive and hands them over to you. Honey oozes warm and sticky between your fingers. Your stomach gurgles with delight.

Pulling a lunch box from his backpack, Guy also collects three frogs he finds beneath the log. You hear them thumping around inside the box the whole walk back to camp.

"You've never eaten roast frog?" Guy says, astonished. "You haven't lived!"

"What does it taste like?" you ask.

"It tastes like frog. A bit like Mexican Walking Fish, maybe. But mainly, it tastes like frog."

You fall asleep with a full stomach to the sound of light rain pattering on the tent canvas.

★

When Guy wakes you at first light, the rain has become a flood. The waters of the swamp have risen up into the tent. Your socks are floating around beside your air mattress. You've been awake ten seconds and you're already cold and damp.

Not that this matters to Guy, who throws open the tent flap. "Treasure awaits!" he declares. "This is when things get really exciting."

Run to page 58.

With a lot of effort, you push open the door. The stone grinds and shivers on its massive hinge. Cool air rushes out to greet you. It's been a long time since anyone walked these floors.

So far, so good. You can make out some hieroglyphs on the wall. Engraved pictures of people, er, dying horribly. Seems this temple was once used for all kinds of cruel and violent acts.

"Those ancient people really were nasty to each other," you mutter to yourself.

As it turns out, those ancient people were pretty nasty to strangers, too. As you step forward, a paving stone shifts beneath your feet. A large circular blade swings out from the wall, slashing at you. This is no time to lose your head!

You're too stunned to duck. All you can do is close your eyes . . .

Nothing happens.

The blade has jammed! The ancient mechanism must be rusty. You can measure the distance from its razor edge to your nose with the tip of one finger.

"Missed by that much," you say, wiping sweat from your forehead. Carefully, you squeeze around the edge of the blade.

But in doing so, you trigger another trap. The floor opens and you tumble into a concealed pit of—soft cushions? Oh. No, these aren't cushions. You've fallen into a teeming mess of huge, angry black *ants*—and they haven't eaten in a long time.

Ants, you think as they start to feast on your juicy skin. *Why did it have to be ants?!*

RUN AGAIN? TURN TO PAGE **8**

As you stand there, looking for another way down the mountain, the demon monkey picks up a large stone and throws it at you.

"Hey!" you shout, diving for the dirt.

The boulder thuds into the ground beside your head. As you struggle to your feet, the demon monkey throws another. This one grazes your shoulder, spinning you around. "Oof!"

You wait to be clobbered by the next one. Lucky for you, the demon monkey has run out of rubble. Looking for another stone, it jumps up onto the ruins of the temple and hurries across to the back wall.

OK, so the demon monkey is the biggest you've ever seen. That doesn't mean it's the smartest. It pulls at the largest stone in the wall and is still pulling when the river bursts through the wall. The demon monkey goes flying.

No longer diverted by the temple's rear wall, the river thunders through the ruins, heading straight for you.

You don't even bother trying to run. Within seconds, you're smacked by a solid wall of water. Somehow you manage to keep hold of the mask and grab onto a fallen tree. The river washes over you, roaring down the overgrown path and doing its best to take you with it.

**To try pulling yourself out of the river,
go to page 109.**

**To let yourself get carried away,
go to page 145.**

You grab the ladder just as the floor collapses beneath you. Guy runs on down the other corridor. You can hear him cheering as he vaults another fallen girder.

"See you up on deck!" he says.

You start climbing the ladder and immediately discover that the rungs are solid, but the wall behind them isn't. A few bolts pull away like bad teeth and the ladder swings free, clobbering you between the eyes. The floor collapses beneath you and you tumble down into the dark belly of the wreck.

You're unconscious before you hit the water. Someone should report this safety violation!

RUN AGAIN? TURN TO PAGE **8**

You chase Guy up and down sloping corridors. Ducking, weaving, and sliding. He's soon kicking in a door marked *Cargo Hold*.

The door crashes from its rotten hinges, opening into a huge chamber. The air in here tastes like pond water.

Guy checks his watch. "Five minutes," he says. "Give or take."

In the center of the hold are two massive piles of suitcases and crates, each wrapped in a rope net. The nets look thick. How long will it take to cut through them?

You hurry toward them but Guy grabs your shoulder. "Hear that?"

The ship creaks and groans, like it's trying to warn you about something. Beneath all that groaning, there's something else. A faint rattle, like rice in a plastic cup.

"What is it?" you ask.

"That's a rattlesnake." Guy whistles. "Deadly. Diamondback, from the sound of it. If one of those sinks its teeth in, you've got a quarter of an hour to get help."

"Snake?!" you say. "I hate snakes!"

The rattle echoes around the shadowy hull, making it impossible to tell exactly where the snake is.

Guy presses forward into the center of the room. You follow gingerly, checking your step. Both nets contain battered cases plastered with stamps from exotic destinations. On the left, these cases are piled atop boxes marked for New York. On the right, the luggage sits on crates of coffee beans destined for Florida. Searching either pile will take two pairs of hands.

"Which one do you want to try first?" Guy says urgently.

**To look for the mask in the Florida pile,
race to page 95.**

**To go through the New York stack,
dash over to page 133.**

You close your eyes and duck down into the cart. You hear the whirr of the wheel, feel the rush of the wind, and hope you've timed this right.

You haven't. *Whoops!*

The wheel's sharp spokes slice you into pieces that will, at least, be easy to send home. You'll definitely save on postage!

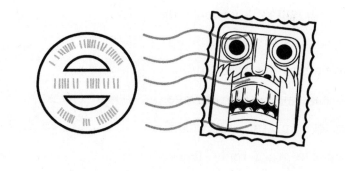

RUN AGAIN? TURN TO PAGE 8

At last, you reach the roof. You see now that the mountain rises higher than the temple. The river starts somewhere near the very top. Once, it probably washed straight down the mountain. Whoever built the temple erected a large stone wall to deflect it down the rock face instead, as a waterfall.

You cup your eyes against the glaring sun and peer up, looking for the river's source. Is that some kind of cave, farther up the mountain? You can see a rocky ledge,  piled with . . . are those bones? You think about those demon monkey legends again.

You climb to the highest point of the roof. There is a large round hole set into it, through which the sun is directed into the temple in a clear, brilliant stream.

You peer down, casting your shadow across a broad stone floor that is engraved with circular

patterns. In the center is a simple stone altar. And on the altar, at the exact point where the sun touches down—can it be? A golden mask!

You've found it!

You're so excited that it takes you several moments to realize that it's a huge drop down to the altar. You might be able to swing down through the hole and climb across the ceiling, but one false move and you're temple pizza.

To swing down through the hole, turn to page 129.

To climb down the mountain and use the front door instead, head to page 78.

You run and slide along steep, sloping corridors. Around you, panels flap loose from walls and ceilings bulge. You hop and skip up sagging staircases, your legs splashing through the rising water. Twice the floor gives way, but each time you leap and keep running.

Finally, you reach the top deck. Again, the ship rocks. You cling to a railing, thinking *this is it*. This time, the wreck really is going to collapse into the swamp.

When nothing happens, you look around for a way down to the muddy banks.

It's raining too heavily to see more than a few feet ahead of yourself. There's no chance of zip-lining down into the swamp. You can barely see any trees.

Looking around for a way out, you notice an ancient lifeboat hanging from a girder overhead. You call out to Guy. "Can we use that?"

"Yeah!" he says, delighted. "Drop down into the swamp, you think?"

The fact that Guy seems so enthusiastic gives you second thoughts.

You crawl up to the portside of the ship and peer down at the swamp. The water is coming up so fast that you won't have time to lower yourself down with the pulley. It's a drop of at least ten yards.

To take the lifeboat, anyway, go to page 31.

If you'd rather head back into the wreck and find a way out through a hole in the side, run to page 127.

Y ou and Barry land, sprawling on the rocky ground. Your cart rockets into the spinning wheel.

A crossbow bolt thuds into the ground beside you. This is no time for lying around. In the moonlight, you can see another opening in the rock face. You point it out to Barry. "We can take shelter there!" you say as he drags himself up.

Ziiiiip! Another bolt flies by your right ear.

"Let's go!" Barry huffs.

You dash to the opening and collapse against the cave wall, out of breath. You shine your flashlight deeper inside. It's a dead end. Turns out this is just a hollow in the rock face, but it does contain a dozen cases of dynamite. This must be where the miners stored their explosives.

Looking back outside, you can still see crossbow bolts sticking out of the ground like stubby saplings.

"Hey, can you hear that?" whispers Barry.

The demon monkey men are chanting, but after a moment you can hear something else, too. Is that water? You shine your flashlight across the rock face at the back of the cave. Sure enough, water is streaming down from a gap in the ceiling. You can see a narrow chasm up there, leading through to a tunnel above.

Barry peers up. "It's too narrow for me, but you might just squeeze through."

Might? You don't like the sound of that.

Barry sees you looking worried. "Hey, no sweat. Maybe we can widen the gap and both get through. I'll just grab some of that dynamite."

Dynamite sounds cool. To move on with a bang, dash to page 144.

To go it alone, head to page 100.

"Lucky I got you away from there, buddy. That boat was bad news."

Barry Bones is driving you back to the island's only town. Spray from the swamp flares in the headlights of his buggy.

You ask him what he means by *bad news*.

"Your friend Scarlett isn't who she says she is. She doesn't work for a museum. She's a spy!"

Huh. That seems kind of exciting. "Who is she spying for?" you ask.

"That's what I'm trying to work out. All I know is, it's some big-shot corporation. We're talking serious money. Word is, they want that mask for its *special properties*."

"What special properties?"

Barry gives you a weird look. "Let's just say people get a bit . . . strange around it."

You're full of questions, but there's only one you care about. "Do you really know where the mask is?"

"You bet I do. The mask *was* on that boat of yours, but thieves beat you to it a long time ago."

Your heart sinks. That wreck has been there for decades. Never mind demon monkeys, thieves have had time enough to find it, strip its treasures, and send them anywhere on the planet. For all you know, the mask is hanging on some private collector's wall on the other side of the world.

Barry seems to read your mind. "Cheer up. My info tells me the robbers didn't get far. They stashed the mask in a nearby mine. I'm not going down there solo. You still want to come with me?"

You glance back. You're sad about missing the wreck but can't help feeling this cop is telling the truth. "I'm with you," you say.

★

The mine is set into a flat-topped hill. The path to the entrance is so overgrown that you and Barry have to leave the buggy halfway up the slope and hack your way through.

To your left, a pulley system takes cartons of coal away down the hill—or did, before the mine was abandoned. At your feet, rusty rail tracks lead into darkness, through a narrow entrance framed by wooden rafters.

You switch on your pocket flashlight. The dark mine seems to swallow up its light. The middle of the night probably isn't the best time to be exploring somewhere like this. And wait—did those bushes over there just rustle? Is someone watching you?

You have a *really* bad feeling about this.

Barry is getting impatient. "You coming or not?"

Some strange gravity is pulling you away from the entrance. Maybe it's that curse Silva spoke about. Entering the mine feels like walking into a haunted house.

But hey, nothing ventured, nothing gained, right? You've come this far . . .

Descend into the mine on page 19.

In your haste, you kick open one of the crates and coffee beans spill out onto the floor. This makes such a loud, whooshing noise that you don't hear the rattlesnake until it's right by your foot. You look down as it sinks its fangs into your ankle.

Ouch! The pain is so intense it nearly knocks your socks off. You swear you can feel the venom sweeping through your veins.

Guy surges forward and snatches you up in his arms. "Don't worry, kid," he says. "We've got twenty minutes to find you some antivenom."

"I thought you said a quarter of an hour," you say. Your leg is already burning up.

"Twenty was me being kind," Guy admits.

Fifteen minutes. As Guy whisks you away along the ship corridors, you already know you'll be late. *Very* late.

RUN AGAIN? TURN TO PAGE **8**

Y ou pull hard on the brake, but it snaps off in your hand. You're accelerating faster than ever!

"Hey, Barry?" You hold the broken brake up to show him.

Barry spins around to see what's going on and the movement knocks the cart down another shaft.

"We're going to have to hold on tight now!" Barry shouts.

You hurtle through darkness. The only light is that from your flashlights and, sometimes, a strange green glow from the tunnel walls. In places, one of the rails has rusted away. You and Barry have to lean the cart up on one wheel to avoid crashing.

At the same time, you're speeding faster and faster. Any moment now, you're going to miss a sharp turn and end up pasted across the mine's wall.

Then—moonlight!

Sighing with relief, you emerge out of the mine onto a short wooden bridge. All too short! Once, coal was dumped here. Today, there's nothing to stop you from sailing off the end of the bridge and crashing to your death on the rocks below.

Aaaaaaaaahhhhh—

This place really needs some health and safety warnings!

RUN AGAIN? TURN TO PAGE 8

Climbing the rock face is harder than it looks. Before long your arms are aching, your fingertips are ragged, and you're scrabbling to find toeholds for your feet.

Every so often, you slip and nearly fall to your death. At least the spray from the waterfall is cool, even if it does make the rocks slippery.

Still, you have to keep going. You've come so far. You try to picture the mask, waiting in the temple. Waiting for *you*.

The screeching cry of some giant animal echoes down the mountain and out across the swamp. You've heard it several times now. Maybe the mask isn't the only thing waiting for you.

Don't think about that. Just keep climbing.

The spray from the waterfall is getting worse. You can barely keep a grip on the rock. Looking left, you notice the water is crashing against a ledge sticking out from the rock face. There's some kind of platform hidden behind the waterfall.

You clamber sideways to the platform. Your

arms sag with relief as soon as your feet touch down. There's a large stone door here, engraved with the image of the mask. It must be a door to the temple.

You press against the door. Some ancient stone mechanism begins to grind within.

Wait. The door isn't *opening*. Instead, the platform beneath your feet is retracting into the cliff face. You clutch at the door, but there's nothing to hold onto. Suddenly, you're standing on nothing. And then you're falling.

You knew you should have learned how to fly!

RUN AGAIN? TURN TO PAGE 8

100

You climb up through the narrow gap. The rock is slippery. You wedge your fingernails into any crack you can find. Whoops! Watch your footing.

"You're doing great!" shouts Barry from below.

It's a long climb. Soon you can't see Barry's flashlight below you. But there's light coming from up above you, a faint green glow. Maybe that's the mask? Barry said it had strange properties.

With the last of your strength you pull yourself up out of the gap into a narrow tunnel.

"I made it!" you shout down to Barry.

When you don't hear anything back, you try shining your flashlight as a signal, but it no longer works.

So where's that green glow coming from?

Turn to page 104.

Creeping across the temple floor, you snatch up the mask. It's heavier than it looks. You're half expecting the altar to sink into the floor, triggering some terrible trap. Shouldn't there be a huge boulder, rolling out from a secret compartment to flatten you into the paving cracks?

"Well done!" Scarlett calls from above. She is peering through the hole in the roof! You wonder how she scaled the temple so quickly. And how she *still* hasn't broken a sweat.

"I'll throw down a rope," she calls. "And then you can bring me the mask."

You look toward the chamber exit behind you. Scarlett notices.

"You do realize this whole temple is one large death trap?" she says. She's still smiling. "To be honest, I wasn't even sure there *was* a safe way to enter. Right now, I'm your best chance of getting out of that room alive."

"And maybe my best chance of never seeing the mask again," you mutter.

Scarlett looks hurt. "I haven't got the foggiest idea what you mean."

A rope drops to the stone floor beside you. Scarlett ties the other end around her waist. "We don't have all day," she says. "This temple has a guardian, you know. Let's get our skates on."

She looks nervous. You remember everything you've heard about demon monkeys and feel a little jittery yourself.

You stare at the mask in your hands. The mask stares back.

If you accept Scarlett's deal, turn to page 105.

To risk the temple's traps, turn to page 135.

You set off for the top deck. Rainwater is flushing down from overhead. The only light you have is the pocket flashlight in your hand, so you don't see the fire hose until it's too late.

The hose has fallen from a reel on the tilted wall and lies across the corridor like a rubbery python. Your boots get tangled in its coils and you smack down hard on the floor. The paneling gives way and you keep falling, down into darkness. All tangled up!

You crash through two more floors before you hit the water. Bad news is the hose comes with you. Its coils wrap snugly around you, pinning your arms to your sides. Looks like you're stuck here for a while! *Bubble, bubble, bubble . . .*

RUN AGAIN? TURN TO PAGE 8

Continuing on down the tunnel, you realize the green glow is phosphorescence—a naturally occurring slime oozing from the rock. That explains the strange smell. The bad news is that the slime only covers a narrow stretch of the shaft. Soon you've moved past it and have to edge into pitch-black. You trip over a rail sleeper and fall flat on your face.

This won't work. You're worried you'll walk straight into a hole. And you can't help feeling there's something spooky waiting in the darkness.

Then you remember that Guy gave you a little cardboard book of matches back at the hotel before you arrived at the swamp. You feel through your pockets. A few coins. A broken flashlight. Success!

You're about to strike a match when you remember that smell. You've left the slime behind, but the stench is worse than ever. If it's *gas*, lighting a match could be a really bad idea.

Still, why stop living dangerously all of a sudden? To strike that match, go to page 108.

Or to push on in the darkness, go to page 116.

"OK, I'll bring you the mask."

Maybe Scarlett is right. The roof probably is the safest way out of this temple.

"Grab the rope!" Scarlett shouts. "We're on a tight schedule here!"

You tuck the mask down the back of your jeans—which feels pretty careless, but it's not like you have a display case on you—and take hold of the rope.

As you start to climb, Scarlett seems relieved. "To think I thought you'd be a problem," she says. "Instead, you've been an absolute asset. If you like, I'll tell—"

Scarlett is cut off mid-sentence by a horrible animal scream. In fact, she's so shocked that she lets the rope unspool in her hands, sending you crashing back down to the stone floor.

It hurts. A *lot*.

"Sorry!" Scarlett yells. You think she's going to

tell you to start climbing again, but she's too busy staring up the mountainside. She looks terrified.

Something crashes down on the roof of the temple. It's a very large something. And very heavy. The ceiling begins to crack and crumble. In a few seconds, the whole thing is going to fall down on top of you.

Through the widening hole in the roof, you catch a glimpse of a dark, hairy body. You sprint for the chamber exit.

Run to page 135.

Whenyoureturntothepath, you're astonished to see Scarlett Fox. "Hello there!" she says, all smiles. "I've missed you!"

She pretends to be surprised to see you, but you get the feeling she was watching you by the waterfall. You had a weird feeling somebody was.

You, on the other hand, are *very* surprised that she's here at exactly the same time as you are. Are you still on the same expedition, technically? Is she still obliged to keep you safe? Why isn't she even slightly sweaty?

"You've done so very well to make it this far," Scarlett says. She tries to make it sound like a compliment, but to you it sounds like a threat. "Why don't you pop down here and we'll join forces?"

You hesitate.

Scarlett looks hurt. "Oh dear. I have the strangest feeling you don't quite trust me."

To go with her up the mountain, head to page 112.

To sprint off alone, run to page 126.

The match flares into life. As the light spreads along the tunnel wall, it reveals two messages scrawled in what looks like red paint. The first says:

BEWARE THE CURSE OF THE MASK!

The second reads:

FEAR THE DEMON MONKEY!

You sigh. Would it have been too much trouble to write: *Mask This Way*? You're wondering what these grim messages mean when—*FLUUMPH!*

That smell *was* gas! Clever you. Bursts of angry flames roar from the tunnel walls, blocking your path, but you can now see a second, much narrower shaft leading off to the left.

You look at those messages again. Someone was definitely trying to warn you off. Which means you must be on the right track with at least one of these tunnels.

To take the main tunnel and try to avoid the jets of fire, turn to page 50.

To squeeze through the shaft, go to page 111.

Clinging onto the fallen tree, you flap around in the fierce current. Try as you might, you can't pull yourself clear of the river. Your head dunks under. *Bubble, bubble, bubble.* You roll over on your back. You kick and fluster.

Before you know it, the demon monkey is standing over you. It no longer seems angry. If anything, it seems amused. You've never seen a giant, skull-faced demon monkey laugh, but there's a first time for everything. You must look pretty funny, squirming away.

The demon monkey plucks you from your log, swings you over one shoulder, and carries you off to a mountain lair. Looking at the piles of neatly polished bones scattered around the rocky ledge,

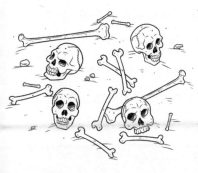

you naturally assume you're on the menu.

Well, you can relax. Waiting at the back of the demon monkey's lair is her young demon monkey son.

He too has a skull face, but on him it looks almost *cute*.

The demon monkey mother points at you, then at her son. She growls something you almost understand. You're to be her son's new playmate, so you'd better start being funny again. *Pronto*.

Know any jokes?

RUN AGAIN? TURN TO PAGE **8**

A few feet into the narrow shaft, you have to drop to your knees and crawl. Thankfully, it's a short tunnel and there's light at the end.

But without warning, you hit a slippery patch. Suddenly, you're sliding headfirst down a tight chute. That circle of light is growing bigger. You can see the end of the tunnel, and then . . . nothing! The tunnel drops into a broad gorge.

You manage to stop yourself from plunging into the fierce river below by flinging out your arms and grabbing the walls of the tunnel. You stop, gasping for air, and peer over the ledge. There's an underground river down there. It pours out through a hole in the rock face. To your right, you see a fragile makeshift bridge, leading over the gorge.

Weirdly, you feel closer than ever to finding that mask. And you're pretty sure that bridge is your best bet. The only question is how quickly to cross.

Do you sprint? Go to page 147.

Or should you try a crawl? Go to page 137.

You decide you and Scarlett can help each other, even if you don't trust each other. It doesn't hurt having another pair of hands to tear through the overgrown path, either. Even better, Scarlett has a small machete in her backpack, which she uses to slice gracefully through the more stubborn obstacles.

"I must say, I'd love to hear more about your adventures," she says. "I would never have imagined you'd have such impressive survival skills." She does actually sound impressed. In fact, she seems so friendly that you find it hard to keep treating her with suspicion. When you tell her how you made it to the mountain, she laughs and gasps in all the right places. In short, she's a perfect audience.

The climb passes a lot more easily than you were expecting. You come around a last bend in the path . . . and there it is, the temple!

The entrance is a large stone face, looking like an even scarier version of the mask. Its evil-looking eyes are inset with green stones that glow in the sunlight. Sharp teeth jut down above the front door. You'll need to walk in through its mouth.

You're about to do so, but Scarlett grabs your elbow. "Let's use those survival skills of yours."

You wonder why she's being so quiet. You're alone here, aren't you?

Scarlett points at a stone grate set in the path, just beneath the entrance. It takes three jabs with her little crowbar to get it open and expose a cramped-looking pipe.

"You want me to crawl in *there*?" you ask.

"You've got the perfect frame to explore this temple," Scarlett says cheerfully. "To be perfectly honest, I'm quite envious."

If you agree to climb in, go to page 11.

If you'd rather use the front door, turn to page 118.

The bee proves hard to follow, darting left and right and ducking in and out of bushes. You and Guy run around, pointing madly every time it buzzes back into view. Guy's having a great time and, as worried as you are about swampy dangers, so are you.

The bee leads you to a marshy area busy with insects. Your bee meets up with some friends. They seem to be burrowing down into the moist earth.

"Jackpot!" Guy exclaims. "Let's get digging!"

Doing your best to push the bees aside, you drive your hands into the earth, pulling up handfuls of mud, until you've created a small well. At the bottom of the hole, water is bubbling up.

"These are Mason bees," Guy explains. "Fresh water is a magnet for these guys. Which makes them a magnet for adventurers like us." He winks.

You fill the collapsible pail with clear water, thinking about food. A few fleshy earthworms are flailing around in the pile of mud you've just created.

"Do you think we could catch a fish?" you ask, looking around for Guy. He's at the edge of the clearing, bent over a fallen log. Bees mill around him, but he seems to be sniffing the bark.

"You'd be more likely to catch an alligator," he says. "And they are way too hard to peel, believe me. I tried cooking a gator in its skin once, like a baked potato. It took three days and it was still cold in the middle."

He stands up, grinning as the buzzing gets louder. "Good news is, I've just found dessert. There's a hive in this log. Should we crack it open?"

What's a little bee sting? To break into the hive for some honey, turn to page 76.

To take your water back to camp and look for food there, turn to page 154.

You edge into the darkness. You can't see anything. If anybody was looking, they wouldn't be able to see you. They also wouldn't be able to see that big hole just behind you. To be fair, you don't see it, either. All you know is the floor has disappeared.

"Aaaahhhhh!"

Your scream bounces around the shaft in much the same way that you do. You hit the ground hard. Ouch!

Wait. Maybe you're not alone. Things are moving in the darkness. The air around you is alive. Whispering. Fluttering.

Something swoops down and bites your neck! Then another something swoops for another bite.

Bats! Vampire bats.

You flail around, trying to scare them away. Unfortunately, they don't seem as scared as you are. You can't fend them off for long, and there's now no way of climbing up the shaft you came down. You can't even see it.

Did these miners never hear about glowing exit signs?

Ah, well. Maybe being swarmed by vampire bats will give you special superpowers. That would be cool. Let's go with that. You're a super-bat hero now. *Yeah.* That's what happens. Not, um, a truly horrible death. Definitely not that.

RUN AGAIN? TURN TO PAGE **8**

"I'm disappointed," Scarlett says. "I thought you were more adventurous than that."

Ouch! But it's a thin line between adventure and recklessness, isn't it? Determined to show you're not afraid, you march up to the front door.

"You're going to just walk in?" Scarlett asks, and you nod.

"Better you than me," she murmurs.

You wonder what she means exactly. Scarlett is standing well back with her arms tightly crossed. Is she using you as a sort of human shield? Maybe that's why she was so eager for you to clamber into that sluice. She wanted to know if it was safe.

"What are you waiting for?" she asks, checking her watch.

The front door looks harmless enough. There are no obvious trip wires or trapdoors. Ah well. Here goes nothing.

Turn to page 78.

Fortunately, the floor holds as you tear up the other corridor. Jumping another fallen girder, you slow down to catch your breath. But right away the ship shudders again, throwing you against the wall.

Guy isn't out of breath at all.

"You can't tell me that wasn't exciting," he says.

"I thought the whole ship was going to collapse on top of us," you say.

"Exactly," Guy says. "By my watch, we've got about ten minutes until the wreck sinks into the mud. Forever."

"Ten minutes?"

Guy mistakes your shock for doubt. "OK," he admits. "So that was me trying to cheer you up. We've got eight minutes, if we're lucky."

Eight minutes to find your treasure? You need a time-out! But you definitely won't get one.

"I say we head straight for the cargo hold," Guy says. "That's all we've got time for. If that mask is anywhere, it'll be there."

You feel the floor tremble again beneath your boots.

"Did I say eight minutes?" Guy says. "I meant six."

Six minutes is no time at all. Barely enough time to make it safely from the ship. Maybe you should forget treasure hunting and just worry about making it out alive.

To head up to the deck and try to find safety, run to page 103.

To look for treasure in the cargo hold, turn to page 83.

You run to the exit. As you do, it grinds open, revealing daylight beyond. Then, just as you're about to charge through, a curved blade swings at you from the wall. But your reflexes are on fire. Without thinking, you drop and slide, scooting out of the temple on your backside.

You have the mask! You're free!

You're so busy being excited about this that you run straight into Scarlett, who is waiting outside the front door. How did she get there?

"Thank you," she says. "You've just saved me a great deal of trouble."

"This is *my* mask," you tell her firmly, "and I'm taking it to a museum—where it belongs!"

Scarlett shakes her head. "That mask is far too valuable for a museum. Hand it over."

You don't move. Hissing with frustration, Scarlett lurches forward and tries to wrench the mask out of your hands.

"We both know it's safer with me!" she shrieks.

"I found it!" you cry.

Behind you, there's a loud rumble. The front wall of the temple has collapsed, and standing atop the rubble is the largest monkey you've ever seen.

It has a weird, skull-like face, as if it's wearing a mask of bone. But that's no mask. And that's no ordinary monkey.

You feel the blood drain from your face. The legends were true. The demon monkey beats its chest and roars, turning your legs to jelly.

Scarlett flees down the path, dropping the mask in her haste. You snatch it up—but which way should you run?

To run after Scarlett, head to page 140.

To find your own escape route, go to page 80.

"**P**ut your hands where I can see them!" you say in your deepest, scariest voice.

The two men ahead of you don't move. At all. They certainly don't shake in their boots. Maybe you need to drop your voice even deeper.

"I *said*, put your hands up," you growl.

The men still don't move. You edge forward.

"I'm aiming for your heads," you say, holding your fingers out like a pretend pistol.

This does the trick. One of the men cleverly drops his head from his shoulders, out of harm's way. It drops all the way to the ground, where it lands with a worrying crack. Ugh.

You're close enough now to see that both of these men are long dead. From the looks of it, they killed each other in a duel.

In fact, it seems that these were the thieves who raided the wreck. Beneath their withered bodies, you find a chest of stolen gems from the *Marie Laveau.* You've found your treasure, but there's no sign of the mask. On the plus side, there's a worn

map stuck to the inside of the chest's lid. It not only shows you a route out of the mine, but highlights a crooked path that leads to a temple, hidden deep in the swamp.

★

By the time you make it back to Barry, there's no sign of the demon monkey men. Instead, the tunnels are full of police.

"Nice haul," Barry says when you show him your treasure. "How are you going to spend it?"

You're not sure. You never imagined you'd end up rich.

"Shame we never found that mask," Barry says. "If it ends up in the wrong hands, there could be trouble."

The police give you a ride back into town. The whole way there, you're thinking about the map. And about Scarlett. And her secret spying. The treasure is amazing, but you can't help feeling you're not done here.

As soon as you can, you leave the treasure in the hotel safe, tuck that map into your back pocket, and head out into the swamp on foot. It takes you most of the morning, but the map is easy to follow. By lunchtime, you're standing on a stony path leading up an overgrown mountain. The wall of the path is engraved with the same mask the demon monkey men were wearing. You can't help but feel you've come to the right place . . .

Take the path to page 29.

126

You sprint away through the undergrowth. Scarlett shouts after you angrily. Never mind.

You find it quicker to dart on and off the path, leaping over or around obstacles instead of trying to tear through them. Finally, you arrive at the top of the mountain. You look back down the slope, but there's no sign of Scarlett. Still, you swear someone—or some*thing*—is moving around in the bushes.

The temple is an impressive stone structure, overrun with moss and vines. The entrance is a terrifying re-creation of the mask, with a heavy door set into its fanged mouth.

You're about to press at the door, but something makes you pause. Maybe it's those stories of a curse. Or all the legends you've read about Egyptian tombs and booby-trapped pyramids. Ancient people were devious and ingenious when it came to protecting their precious things from treasure hunters.

You could always climb up the wall and try the roof. Run to page 86.

But the front door *is* right there . . .
You could go to page 78.

Running back down the corridors, your boots slip. Heavy rain cascades down the sloping floors. You land on your back and water sweeps you away down the corridor. Maybe that's for the best. You don't have time to run. Any minute now, the rain will tear this ship apart.

"Woo-hooooo!" Guy whizzes past you on the seat of his pants, holding the trunk of treasure above his head.

You follow his lead, using the flooded floors as a water slide. You skim and slip along corridors and down stairwell waterfalls, heading back into the belly of the wreck. You have to duck collapsed girders and paddle yourself around corners, but you start to get the hang of it. If this wasn't so dangerous, it would be great fun!

Still, you start to worry you're going too fast.

You shout at Guy: "Shouldn't we be looking for a way out?"

"Let gravity show us a way out!" he shouts back. "All this water has to be going somewhere!"

You wonder if this is the sort of thinking that makes people go over Niagara Falls in a barrel. Something you've never wanted to do.

Guy said this wreck had ten minutes left. That was about twenty minutes ago. You need to get off this ship, *fast*.

To grab hold of something and look for an exit, turn to page 53.

To keep sliding after Guy, turn to page 25.

You carefully lower yourself through the hole. This would be a really bad time to slip. You'd be meeting the mask headfirst, in way too much of a rush.

The curved ceiling is held up by wooden beams. There's just enough of an edge to cling onto one of them and so, hand over hand, one leg in front of the other, you clamber down to the floor. Almost like an ancient dance of hokey pokey.

Climb down to page 101.

You follow Guy's lead and swing down quickly through the trees. The demon monkey crashes through the trees behind you.

You swing, you jump, you swing again. Soon you're halfway down the mountain.

Then—disaster! As you swing out from a treetop, the mask comes loose from the belt of your jeans. It spins through the air in front of you and you snatch blindly at it with one hand. You just manage to hook a finger through and clutch it back to your chest.

Lucky. But you've lost your momentum. In that split second the demon monkey has caught up, and is now waiting for you to swing right into its open jaws. Luckily, Guy lurches over, grabs you by the leg, and pulls you to safety.

"Caught you!" he says, winking.

He swings off to the next tree with a whoop. You follow, tree to tree, just mere seconds ahead of the huffing, roaring demon monkey.

At last, you crash down in the final tree, a hair in front of the beast. Guy is waiting at the base of its trunk, revving the swamp buggy's engine. "Jump!"

You drop into the passenger seat and Guy slams his foot down on the accelerator. Just in time, too. The tree collapses under the demon monkey's weight. The beast somersaults and belly flops down into the swamp.

As you burn off into the distance, you see the demon monkey struggling with a pack of hungry gators.

Guy looks over at you. The mask is resting on your lap, glaring up with its empty eyes. "That's some treasure," he says. "Where are we taking it?"

You're surprised. "Don't you work for Scarlett?"

"You won't catch me working for anybody, kid. I was just in this for the adventure. So where to?"

You consider. Part of you isn't ready to think about letting go of the mask. Not after all the trouble you've been to getting hold of it.

"I should take it to Barry Bones," you say, trying to sound surer than you feel. "He'll make sure it goes to a museum. That's where I want it to end up."

Surprisingly, Guy agrees. "Good call. You know, there's a whole world of lost treasures out there. If you've got a taste for exploring, next week I'm off to—"

You nod along as Guy outlines his next great adventure. It sounds tempting. But right now you can't take your eyes off your treasure. You have a weird feeling the mask doesn't want you to say good-bye.

Maybe you don't really *have* to give it to Barry. It is yours, after all. Wouldn't it be a waste to see it locked up in some dusty old museum? After everything you've been through, you reason, maybe you *deserve* a memento.

If nothing else, you might need proof that all this craziness really happened.

To hand the mask over to Barry, go to page 70.

To keep it for yourself, sneak off to page 149.

Guy slices through the netting of the New York pile and you both snatch up cases and empty their contents at your feet. Soon you're standing in a mess of moldy old clothes. You almost give up the search. Is there still time to make it off the wreck before it collapses on top of you?

"We've got about three minutes," Guy says, as if reading your mind. Then he presses a finger to his lips. "Wait." He spins around, knife in hand. The rattlesnake is sliding across the floor toward you. Guy throws his weapon, almost casually, and the blade neatly pins the snake to the floor.

"OK, two and a half minutes," he says.

One last case and you're out of here. You heave up a crocodile-skin suitcase and there beneath it is a wooden trunk. It looks *really* old, and you get the feeling it's been hidden at the center of the pile.

You pry open the lid. The trunk is packed with gold doubloons and gems. They glitter and gleam in the light from your flashlight. It's not the mask, but it's still—

"Treasure!" Guy says, beaming. "You're rich!"

Without another word, he swings the trunk up on his shoulder and takes off across the room. As you follow, you feel the ship shake and tilt again. You fall to the floor, which is now at forty-five degrees. It's going to be a steep climb to the top deck.

"Maybe we should find another hole in the side and jump down?" you say, looking at the ceiling and waiting for it to fall. Water is starting to gush through widening cracks.

Guy shakes his head. "Best we keep heading up. With a bit of luck, we can zip-line down from the deck."

You're not sure how much luck you have left. You're at least three floors from the top deck. And you have slightly less than two minutes until the whole wreck collapses.

To look for a quicker way out, go to page 127.

To try to reach the deck, dash to page 88.

You sprint out of the chamber, the mask heavy in your hands. Something in the floor clicks beneath your feet. A burst of flame jets across the passage in front of you.

"Whoa!"

You manage to slide beneath it, clutching the mask to your chest.

Another roar echoes down the corridor after you. There is a loud crash and the floor rocks. Something very large and very nasty has just landed on the spot where the altar used to be. Now, there's only rubble.

You don't dare look back. Which is just as well, as a spiked hammer swings out at you from a wall. You breathe in and dart to the right. It misses you, but not by much.

Keep running. Don't look back.

Wait. Is the floor moving? Yes. The floor is parting down the middle. A rusted saw comes spinning up at you. You leap across it like an Olympian long jumper and crash down, nearly losing your balance. But you keep running—with both your legs.

The whole temple is shaking now. Something is chasing you, tearing the place apart as it runs.

Don't look back.

Ahead of you is a large stone door. If your sense of direction is right, it must be the *front* door.

You're nearly out of here! But wait—maybe this is too easy.

Imagine you were an ancient, devious trap-maker. Wouldn't you booby-trap the front door?

To look for another exit, go to page 138.

To risk it, turn to page 121.

This is one rickety bridge. Far too rickety. Even though you're crawling carefully, it starts to break apart. Board after board plunges toward the rushing water below—and soon you do, too!

Aaaaaaaaah!

At least you left your mark on the world. Or on that rickety bridge, anyway!

RUN AGAIN? TURN TO PAGE **8**

Another corridor peels off to the left. You take it, trying not to listen to the thundering footsteps right behind you.

Too late, you realize this corridor is a dead end. And you're running too fast to slow down. On the plus side, you might knock yourself unconscious before you're caught by whatever is chasing you.

At the last second, the wall pulls back. It's a door!

"Kid?" Guy Dangerous is standing on the other side of the wall, as surprised as you are. He looks battered, sweaty, and very happy.

"Run!" you shout. "Something's coming!"

Guy frowns, peering down the dark corridor behind you. "I don't see anything. You haven't been eating those yellow swamp berries, have you?"

You spin around, gasping for air, but—he's right. The temple is still shaking, but there's nothing chasing you. Maybe you lost it?

You show Guy the golden mask. He looks impressed, whistling and ruffling your hair. Then he tells you he's climbed up the mountain through the treetops. Just for fun. "I saw the temple from the swamp and thought, what the heck!"

You can see a series of ropes leading down through the trees to the foot of the mountain. You're relieved. You want to get as far away from this temple as you can, and quickly.

"We need to get the mask to safety," you tell him.

"Safety? I don't see anything dangerous. And I should know, because my—" Guy is drowned out by an unearthly roar that seems to shake the temple. Looking up, you find the biggest monkey you've ever seen, standing atop the roof. It bellows right at you, flinging back your hair like a gale-force wind. You have the distinct, horrible impression that this demon monkey won't rest until it gets its mask back.

"OK," Guy gulps. "Follow me." He swings off back the way he came. You pause a moment, torn.

Do you follow Guy and swing through the trees? Head to page 130.

Or do you try giving the demon monkey its mask back? Turn to page 156.

140

You stumble along the overgrown path, the mask heavy in your hand, glimpsing Scarlett's red hair through the trees. How *does* she move so fast?

The demon monkey is even faster. You feel the earth shake as it pounds after you. You turn back to see how close it is. That was a mistake. For one thing, the demon monkey is way closer than you want it to be. For another, it means you don't notice a sharp turn in the path. You crash to the floor and wind up flat on your back. *Oof.* Man down!

The demon monkey looms above you, blocking out the sunlight. It rips the mask out of your hands and bellows in triumph.

Maybe the demon monkey will forget about you now that it has its prize. That would be nice. But demon monkeys *aren't* nice. All you can hope for is that you give the big hairy beast a real stomachache.

Chomp!

RUN AGAIN? TURN TO PAGE 8

You can handle three jets of flame, you think. Counting down, you take a running jump and fling yourself into the air.

This is the exact moment when three more jets of flame explode from the tunnel floor.

The heat must be widening the cracks, you reason.

Even at the end, you're pretty bright.

Shame you've been burned to a crisp.

Does anyone smell toast?

RUN AGAIN? TURN TO PAGE 8

You take a deep breath and launch yourself out over the murky water. You're sure you see the beady eyes of a gator watching you from below, thinking of its next meal. This is one time you definitely don't want a soft landing.

A second later, you crash down hard in the belly of the dinghy. The boat is still rocking as you jump to your feet and tug hard at the outboard motor's pull cord. Once. Twice. Three times.

Finally, the motor chokes, splutters, and roars. You drop down into the seat and turn the bow around to face the open swamp. You can see the red brake lights of the buggy leaving trembling trails across the dark water.

The dinghy moves quickly. Soon you're gaining on Silva.

"Don't try to follow me, *amigo!*" he shouts, seeing that he's no longer alone. "It will be very dangerous for you."

He's not wrong. Silva steers the buggy into the swamp, bumping through mangroves and over a high bank. You don't see the bank until it's too late to turn back. You rev the outboard motor, building up as much speed as you can, before—

Thwack!

The dinghy bounces up the slope and vaults into the air. You duck as a tree swings out at you in the darkness and hold on tight as the dinghy drops down hard onto the water.

Silva was counting on losing you. Instead, you've nearly caught up to him. Another burst of speed from the motor and suddenly you're side by side with the buggy. Could this be your best chance of getting back the treasure?

If you jump now, you could have a chance to overpower Silva. Leap to page 67.

But it's a dangerous jump. If you take a second to steady yourself, turn to page 72.

It doesn't take Barry long to rig the dynamite. "Better stand back, buddy," he warns you. "This is going to be one big bang."

He isn't wrong. What Barry doesn't know is that there's a strong seam of coal gas behind that rock face. As soon as he lights the fuse, the gas ignites and creates an explosion loud enough to be heard in Antarctica. Your ears would be ringing for weeks. If you still *had* ears. As it is, your ears, nose, and toes are scattered from here all the way to the swamp. Talk about going out with a bang!

RUN AGAIN? TURN TO PAGE 8

You let go of the tree and are whisked away by the fast-flowing river. The water has turned the stone path into a twisting set of rapids, strewn with obstacles. You have to paddle desperately to avoid a boulder in the middle of the path. Seconds later, you've no choice but to hold your breath and duck underwater to avoid a massive log.

At least you've left the monkey behind you, right? Wrong! The beast is bounding down the mountain beside the path, ripping out bushes and trees as it goes. When you back-paddle to avoid a collapsed section of wall, the monkey's claws slash down to try to fish you out. You dive underwater and the monkey misses.

After that, you let the river take you wherever it wants. Soon, the monkey can't keep up. You hear its howls of frustration as you disappear around yet another bend.

On and on you tumble, until finally you're washed out into the swamp. The current ebbs and you're able to swim back to shore before any gators notice you. It feels good to be on solid ground.

You hold the mask up in front of you. "Well," you tell it, "thanks for the ride. But I think it's time we got you locked up somewhere safe."

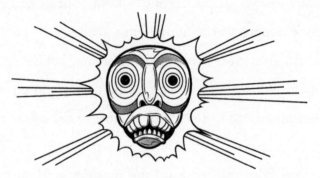

Turn to page 70.

You sprint along the narrow bridge. It immediately starts trembling, and then boards beneath your feet start to shatter, tumbling into the gorge below.

Yikes! You leap through the air to whatever boards are left, desperately trying to avoid tumbling into the river below.

Just as you reach the other side, the last of the bridge crumbles away. You smack into the rocky ledge, knocking the air from your chest. Still, you're alive.

You hang there for a moment, then pull yourself up. You look down and see the wooden boards snapping and splintering in the river's white water.

There's another tunnel here, much wider than the last. Without thinking, you strike a match to see into the tunnel ahead of you. And what you see is the outline of two men.

You freeze, and your match instantly goes out.

More monkey men? You hold your breath, but you don't hear anything.

To your left is a dark nook. Should you hide in there and see what happens, or brave up and confront the men?

To hide, turn to page 116.

To confront the men, go to page 123.

Guy drops you back in town. "Remember," he says, "there are lots more adventures where this one came from. Look me up." Then he speeds away, the buggy fishtailing in the dirt.

Barry is waiting for you in the hotel lobby. He raises his eyebrows. "You look like you were dragged through a bush backward."

"I should head up to my room and pack," you say.

Barry narrows his eyes. "Thought maybe you got lucky. With the mask, I mean." He stares right into you. It's like he can read the truth scrawled across your heart, even as you tell a big, dirty lie.

"Nope," you say, and hurry off.

Upstairs in your room, you wrap the mask in your dirty laundry.

The whole journey home, you're waiting for an airport alarm to go off or for a heavy hand on your shoulder. But you get away with it. You smuggle the mask all the way back to your bedroom.

Well done. Now you'll always have a reminder of this great adventure! You spend your first day back at home gazing at it happily, feeling sure you did the right thing by keeping it for yourself.

But when your parents see the mask on your bedroom wall, they're *not* happy. They can't afford to insure a priceless treasure, and word is bound to get out that this mask is in your possession. What happens if someone tries to steal it?

You lie awake at night, worried that masked men will hunt you down for your treasure. Soon, you're convinced you're being followed around town. And then there's the creepy graffiti you keep seeing in your neighborhood. All those scrawled slogans about **DEMON MONKEYS** and **THE CURSE OF THE MASK**.

Finally one night, you look out your bedroom window and a skull-faced demon monkey is looking in. You get the feeling it's not here for some milk and cookies. *Adios!*

RUN AGAIN? TURN TO PAGE **8**

With the thieves in pursuit, you and Barry sprint off down the right-hand shaft.

"We need to lose these guys!" Barry shouts.

Ahead, the tunnel forks again. Barry leads you down the left shaft and ducks into a hollow in the wall. Squeezing in beside him, you press your face against the cold stone.

A few seconds pass. You hold your breath. Then there's a shuffling of feet and whispered words. The monkey men are at the fork in the shaft, trying to decide which way to go.

A flash of lantern light bounces across the walls of your tunnel. A few of the men creep past. They walk right by without seeing you!

Your lungs are about to burst.

A few seconds later, the men return. They seem to be laughing behind their masks. At the fork, they run off with their comrades down the other tunnel.

"Those are some blind sons of monkeys," Barry chuckles. "We got really lucky there."

"Why were they laughing?" you ask.

He shrugs. "Who knows what goes on in those monkey brains?"

You step out of the hollow and freeze. You can hear crackling. Is it coming from the roof? As you look up, soot spits in your eye.

"Well now, will you look at that?" Barry is shining his flashlight down the shaft. There's a glint of gold in the rocky floor. Hurrying over, you snatch it up. It's a gold doubloon. You spot another, a bit farther on. And then another! And another!

Soon you and Barry are running, taking it in turns to snatch up the coins. You hurtle around a corner and grind to a halt. The tunnel has come to an abrupt end. But there, against the far wall, is a treasure chest. An actual treasure chest! The sort of thing pirates drew maps about.

"This is it!" Barry exclaims. "This is where they hid the mask!"

"But where did the coins come from?" you ask.

Barry doesn't seem to hear. He takes a deep breath and opens the chest. It's packed with gold doubloons and bright green jewels.

"Wow!" you gasp.

"Hang on, that looks like a note." Barry heaves the chest up and slides out a neatly folded square of paper from underneath.

It says: **¡UNA MUERTE FELIZ!**

He reads it aloud. "That's Spanish. Hmm, I think it means, *A happy death*. But why—?"

You don't have to wonder for long. Behind you, the roof of the tunnel collapses in a cascade of rocks and coal. It's a trap! You've been sealed in.

"Guess now we know why those monkey men were laughing," you say.

Buried alive. Still, at least you'll die stinking rich!

RUN AGAIN? TURN TO PAGE **8**

You return to camp pretty much empty-handed. The best snack Guy can come up with is a fistful of worms you'd hoped to use for fish bait.

"Full of nutrition," Guy promises, throwing the worms on a skillet over an open fire. "And loaded with good bacteria. Also loaded with bad bacteria, but it should all balance out."

He hands you a steaming plate of the slippery things, and they taste just as disgusting as they look.

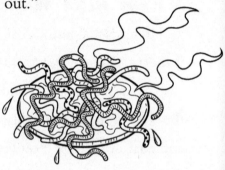

Guy falls asleep instantly after dinner, but you lie awake, listening to the cries of mysterious creatures. At one point, you hear a bellowing roar and sit bolt upright in bed. After a few moments, you decide the scream isn't human. That doesn't cheer you up.

Gurgle.

What was that?

Gurgle gurgle.

It seems to be coming from inside the tent!

Gurrrrgle.

It's your stomach! Those worms must still be writhing around in there. You're going to be sick. You feel around in the darkness for a container, but you don't find one. In the end, you have to run out of the tent to the water's edge and throw up. Food poisoning is the worst.

No, wait. Being eaten alive by an alligator is much worse than that. Guess you should have made sure the coast was clear before you came running from the tent. It's feeding time! Good-bye, brave explorer. Hello, gator food.

RUN AGAIN? TURN TO PAGE **8**

Y ou hold out the mask to the demon monkey.
It isn't interested. Maybe it's waiting for an
apology.

"Hey, I'm really sorry," you say. "I, uh, didn't
know it was yours." You don't sound very convincing.

The demon monkey reaches down, grabs you by
the back of your shirt, and shoves your head into its
mouth.

It's very dark in here. And wet. And smelly.
Thankfully, you're not going to be in here for long.
Looks like this demon monkey eats explorers like
you for breakfast!

RUN AGAIN? TURN TO PAGE **8**